BY ROBERT KINERK

OH, HOW SYLVESTER CAN PESTER!

PICTURES BY DRAZEN KOZJAN

And Other Poems More or Less About Manners

A Paula Wiseman Book
Simon & Schuster Books for Young Readers
New York London Toronto Sydney

To my well-mannered
brothers and sisters:
Maureen, Dick, Mary, Joe,
Mike, and Katy—R. K.

For Alison, my good-mannered
and loving sweetie, and Monty—D. K.

SIMON & SCHUSTER BOOKS FOR YOUNG READERS
An imprint of Simon & Schuster Children's Publishing Division
1230 Avenue of the Americas, New York, New York 10020
Text copyright © 2011 by Robert Kinerk
Illustrations copyright © 2011 by Drazen Kozjan
SIMON & SCHUSTER BOOKS FOR YOUNG READERS is a trademark of Simon & Schuster, Inc.
For information about special discounts for bulk purchases, please contact
Simon & Schuster Special Sales at 1-866-506-1949 or business@simonandschuster.com.
The Simon & Schuster Speakers Bureau can bring authors to your live event.
For more information or to book an event, contact the Simon & Schuster Speakers Bureau
at 1-866-248-3049 or visit our website at www.simonspeakers.com.
Book design by Lucy Ruth Cummins
The text for this book is set in Artcraft.
The illustrations for this book are rendered digitally.
Manufactured in China
1210 SCP
2 4 6 8 10 9 7 5 3 1
Library of Congress Cataloging-in-Publication Data
Kinerk, Robert.
Oh, how Sylvester can pester! : and other poems more or less
about manners / Robert Kinerk ; illustrated by Drazen Kozjan.
p. cm.
"A Paula Wiseman Book."
ISBN 978-1-4169-3362-5 (hardcover)
1. Courtesy—Juvenile poetry. 2. Etiquette—Juvenile poetry.
3. Children's poetry, American. I. Kozjan, Drazen, ill. II. Title.
PS3561.I455O38 2011
811'.6—dc22
2010000771

first
edition

Contents

MANNERS!

Who needs them?

I don't think *I* do.

Whenever they're mentioned, what I do is boo.

How awful. How terrible. How horrible. How grim,

to make me be someone all proper and prim.

You need them though, you rascally tyke.

They'll help you to treat me the way that I like,

and not hurt my feelings, and not make me sore,

or make me downhearted, and much, much, much more.

So as a concession, here's what I'll do:

You be nice to me; I'll be nice to you.

That agreement might work. It may get us quite far.

(And it *could* be what manners, in truth, really are.)

CLEAN YOUR ROOM

When you hear someone yelling, "Get this room clean!"

Calmly but firmly ask, "What do you mean?

The box that held cookies in crinkly paper?

The juice that's been spilled and requires a scraper?

The Frisbee I left where it happened to fall?

Or the bat? Or the mitt? Or the hat? Or the ball?

Or the thingamajig that I found at the dump,

or the chocolate bar melted now into a lump?

Or is it the fact you must squeeze through my door,

that's now hard to open because on the floor

I've dropped all the shirts and the shorts and the pants

that belong in the wash? Or is it the ants

that have filed from somewhere and more or less wandered

through all of that clothing that ought to be laundered?

Well, then, *okay*! If it's *that* that you mean,

then maybe you're right, and perhaps I should clean."

WHAT WILL HAPPEN TO YOU IF YOU TALK WHILE YOU CHEW?

First you'll hear cries of dismay and disgust.

You'll be heckled and booed. You'll be cursed and be cussed.

You'll be yanked from your seat. You'll be rushed out the door.

Your family will bellow, "The horror! Oh, the horror!"

They'll call you a pig and they'll call you a slob.

Your mother will faint and your sisters will sob.

Your brother will yell that you're making him sick.

From your cat and your dog what you hear will be, "Ick!"

So . . .

To avoid that pain and that grief and that shock,

when your mouth's full of food—*remember*—don't talk!

AT THE MOVIES

Talkers in movies! We ought to collect them
and seat them in seats that pop up and eject them.
And even those in nearby rows
who crinkle their candy bar wrapping
ought to be led to an alley or shed
and tied up with twine or with strapping.

There ought to be armies of top-notch, trained booers
protesting those loudmouths disturbing us viewers.
Or the star on the screen should step down in mid-scene
and capture a sneezer who's spraying,
and rough up the lout and hustle him out,
then go back to the role he's been playing.
At least that's the way I think things ought to be
unless that disturber in movies is *me*!

THE GIGGLES

One of the things that all kids have to dread
is getting the giggles at something that's said,
when giggling's not something someone should do.
For instance, when someone is lecturing you.
Or say there's this concert. It's played in a park.
You're there with a friend, and some sort of spark—
something quite small, let's say—has occurred,
as slight as a glance or as slight as a word,
and it suddenly seems like you'll split right in half
unless you let out this big, rip-roaring laugh.
You're pressing your hands right away to your lips
in case there's a chance something giggly slips.
Your friend will be doing the same thing as you,
for the giggles are worse when the fit has struck two.
You laugh till you're practically weeping, and then . . .
you glance at your friend and it all starts again!

MAY I INTERRUPT?

When someone is speaking—a grown-up, let's say—
can you interrupt? In general, no way.
There're exceptions to that, but they're rare.
They occur in those instances where
lightning is flashing its bolts from the sky
and they'd land on your friend, or at least land nearby,
or a hive's been disturbed and the bees, in their wrath,
are aimed at your friend in a bullet-straight path.
In cases of bees or a bolt from the blue,
you *may* interrupt. In fact, dear, please do!

7

SHAKE HANDS

They offer their hand, and that's all you can see.

If you're short, you come up to an inch past their knee.

But even if not, unless they have knelt,

your head will be level, at best, with their belt.

They offer their hand and it's bony.

In color it's much like baloney.

Or red as a brick. Or skinny. Or thick.

Or squishy like cooked macaroni.

They offer their hand, and you hear yourself told,

"Oh my, aren't you big! And now you're how old?"

And if you don't speak, if you gulp or you choke,

your mother or father will give you a poke.

They offer their hand and you take it and shake.

And your fingers don't wilt. And your arm doesn't break.

You say what you should when your parents' friends greet you.

Speaking politely, you say, "Nice to meet you."

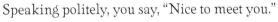

You *like* it, you find, and it's not long before
you're telling your parents, "Line up some more!"
"Line up your friends or pure strangers," you shout.
Forward you rush with your hand sticking out.
And the rest of the day, on street after street,
you greet and you greet and you greet and you greet.

ELEANOR ICKITY

Oh how persnickety, Eleanor Ickity!
There's nothing she's served that she likes.

You can offer her fish on a parsley-lined dish
and she'll turn up her nose and shriek,

You'll hear little Ellie shriek, "Yikes!"
For Ellie is one of those tykes

whose list is quite ample of things she won't sample.

Serve her a dish of chopped corn!
She'll weep that she ever was born.

Till a glance from her mother or father
reminds her she's being a bother

and they'd like it a lot if their finicky tot
would have the politeness and grace
to sample at least a small trace.

Finally young Ellie relents.
But she says as she nods and consents,

"I wouldn't be nearly as cranky and cross
if you topped this corn off with some nice chocolate sauce."

Chocolate on servings of corn
is something her parents both scorn.

And they tell her, "How dumb,"
while they're serving her some.
But Ellie won't listen and Ellie won't wait.

She rapidly, rapidly fills up her plate,

then digs in and bellows,

YUM!
YUM!

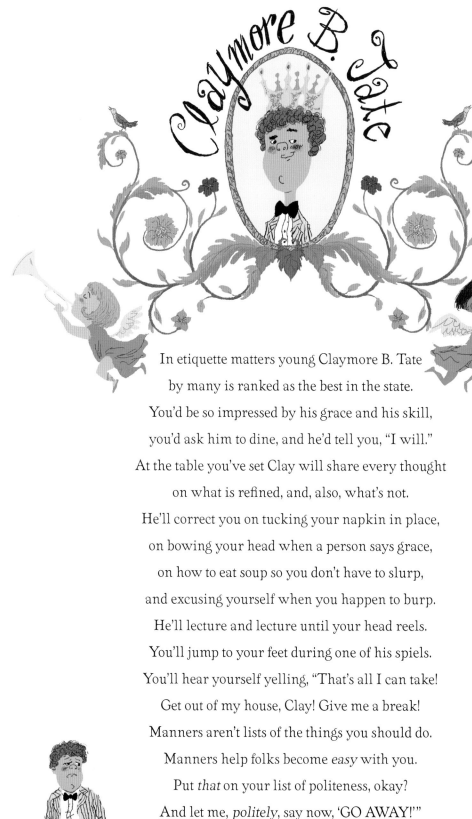

Claymore B. Tate

In etiquette matters young Claymore B. Tate
by many is ranked as the best in the state.
You'd be so impressed by his grace and his skill,
you'd ask him to dine, and he'd tell you, "I will."
At the table you've set Clay will share every thought
on what is refined, and, also, what's not.
He'll correct you on tucking your napkin in place,
on bowing your head when a person says grace,
on how to eat soup so you don't have to slurp,
and excusing yourself when you happen to burp.
He'll lecture and lecture until your head reels.
You'll jump to your feet during one of his spiels.
You'll hear yourself yelling, "That's all I can take!
Get out of my house, Clay! Give me a break!
Manners aren't lists of the things you should do.
Manners help folks become *easy* with you.
Put *that* on your list of politeness, okay?
And let me, *politely*, say now, 'GO AWAY!'"

BRUSSELS SPROUTS

"Brussels sprouts," said Mother White.

"Chauncey, dear, try just one bite."

In reply, her offspring wrote

the following poetic note:

"Concerning the vegetable brussels sprouts

children rightly have their doubts.

In looks it's like a cabbage shrunk.

Its odor would alarm a skunk.

To see it steaming on a plate

produces groans and rage and hate.

Oh, parents, pity your poor tot

and leave the brussels sprouts unbought."

His father took the note. He read.

He gave it thought, and then he said,

"This poem is terrific, son. Nothing can beat it.

As for your vegetable, though, Chauncey—eat it!"

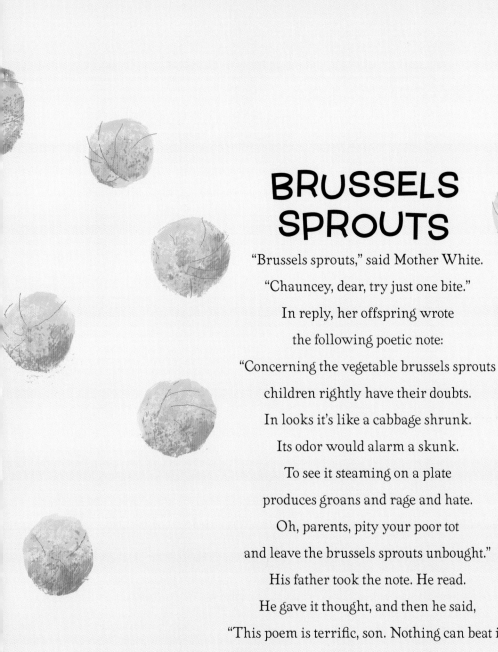

MAGIC WORDS

One day at lunch (macaroni and cheese)
Principal Plunk forgot to say "please."
A hush filled the room and everyone stared.
Should he be corrected? No! No one dared.
Though Lulu and Tank and Marshall and Clem
covered their mouths and said softly, "Ahem."
Which Principal Plunk took at once as a clue,
there was something he might have forgotten to do.
Our sweet, our polite, our poor Principal Plunk,
he thunk and he thunk and he thunk and he thunk.
He paced and he pondered and scratched his bald head
till he finally remembered and gleefully said,
"Oh yes, for my lunch (macaroni and cheese),
when I said, 'Fill my plate,' I should have said 'please.'"
The children all cheered, and then from their ranks,
came a *second* reminder: "And now you say 'thanks.'"

OH, HOW SYLVESTER CAN PESTER!

In the art of the screech, Sylvester's the best.

He's enormously talented, gifted, and blessed.

With his jugular vein hugely swelling his neck out,

he'll scream, "I want *that*!" to his mom at the checkout.

His lungs fill with air, and he lets out a screech

that breaks all the objects of glass within reach.

Oh, how Sylvester can pester!

However, in terms of mosquito-like whines,

the talented, lovely Belle Popworthy shines.

Her whine seems to linger. Her whine seems to swell.

What a *genius* at whines, that persistent young Belle.

And you hope that Sylvester and Belle someday meet.

And she gives her whine, and he gives his bleat.

And they both fall in love and rush off hand in hand.

And silence at last is restored to the land!

15

SAMMY T. SARDY

It gives me no pleasure, but I have to state,

Sammy T. Sardy again is quite late.

Our whole class is waiting. We're sitting in rows.

And Sammy, at home, is still not in his clothes.

Our kind, patient teacher, Miss Mildred McCarty,

calls out very loudly the name of Sam Sardy.

She calls out his name, but young Sam isn't there.

He's still in his bedroom. He's combing his hair.

Our class heaves a sigh. Our eyes start to roll,

as Sammy, at home, fills his cereal bowl.

He's put on his jacket, but he's yet to zip.

And today is the day that our class takes a trip.

Yes, the class takes a trip that we're all eager for,

and Sammy's just now walking out of his door.

At leisure he slowly strolls up to the bus,
which dear Miss McCarty has now filled with us.
The driver is waiting. He's tapping his foot.
What he has to say is extremely well put:
"Sammy T. Sardy! Oh, Sammy T. Sardy,
what is the reason, my boy, you're so tardy?"
"I'm sorry, of course," says Sammy T. Sardy.
"But here I am now. And now let's depart-y."
And *"Oh!"* we all go, "Oh, that Sammy T. Sardy!"

STOP CROWDING

All

        sneaking

in

line

and

all

    crowding,

no doubt,

makes

people

behind

yell,

"Hey, you,

get

. . . . OUT!"

TICKETS

18

EXCUSE ME

If you burp,

if you slurp,

say, "Excuse me."

If you spill

(and you will),

say, "Excuse me."

You *will* make mistakes.

When you do—goodness' sakes!

You can make it okay

if you simply will say,

EGBERT

Egbert dropped his underwear
here and there—he didn't care.
The same with pants and shirt and shoes.
The things he dropped he'd tend to lose,

20

and 'cause his wardrobe was quite small,
soon he had no clothes at all.
Now, when he's seen, there comes this hush.
I can't say why or else I'll blush.

SHOE POLISH

Chuck took a bath

and then shined his shoes,

a pattern of duties

no one should choose.

For the polish that gave
his shoes so much charm

left its mark on his knees,

and his nose,

and one arm.

So when he had given

his shoes their last rub,

SNAP

his mother yelled,

"You!
Get back in that tub!"

SNEEZES

A sneeze from Louise is more than a breeze.

It's like a typhoon in its power.

The blast whistles past. It leaves you aghast.

You're shaking for more than an hour.

You can't find your jacket.

You can't find your comb.

You notice she's knocked down the walls of your home.

Gone is your fence.

Gone is your gate.

Your roof has been found in a neighboring state.

You peer in your closet.
You can't find your clothes
And you're wondering, *Where could my shoes be?*
Meanwhile, of course, the source of this force
politely is saying, "Excuse me."

AT THE TABLE

Children, dear, whenever able,
keep your elbows off the table.
Your other joints also, please,
such as your ankles and your knees.
Furthermore, make sure your heels
don't leave prints on Papa's meals.
"Alas!" you'd hear your parents cry
should they someday glance up and spy

a daughter, doing pirouettes,

tipping over vinaigrettes,

or a male offspring playing hoops

and splashing through the family's soups.

Your mom would sigh. Your dad would say,

"That wasn't done, not in *my* day!"

27

THE
SECRET

When you think about manners, there seem to be lots—
like what you should do and what you should *not*.
Don't worry about it; it's not a big deal.
What should matter to you is the way that you feel.
Feel good. Feel glad. Feel proud. Feel right.
And the secret to that is to just be polite.